Zach Gets Some Exercise

By Sarah, Duchess of York

Illustrated by Ian Cunliffe

STERLING CHILDREN'S BOOKS

New York

STERLING CHILDREN'S BOOKS
New York

An Imprint of Sterling Publishing
387 Park Avenue South
New York, NY 10016

STERLING and the distinctive Sterling logo are registered trademarks of
Sterling Publishing Co., Inc.

Library of Congress Cataloging-in-Publication Data Available

Lot#:
2 4 6 8 10 9 7 5 3 1
03/11
Published by Sterling Publishing Co., Inc.
387 Park Avenue South, New York, NY 10016
www.sterlingpublishing.com/kids
Story and illustrations © 2007 by Startworks Ltd.
"Ten Helpful Hints" © 2009 by Startworks Ltd.
Distributed in Canada by Sterling Publishing
c/o Canadian Manda Group, 165 Dufferin Street
Toronto, Ontario, Canada M6K 3H6
Distributed in Australia by Capricorn Link (Australia) Pty. Ltd.
P.O. Box 704, Windsor, NSW 2756, Australia

Sterling ISBN 978-1-4027-7399-0

For information about custom editions, special sales, premium and
corporate purchases, please contact Sterling Special Sales
Department at 800-805-5489 or specialsales@sterlingpublishing.com.

All children face many new experiences as they grow up, and helping them to understand and deal with each is one of the most demanding and rewarding things we do as parents. Helping Hand Books are for both children and parents to read, perhaps together. Each simple story describes a childhood experience and shows some of the ways in which to make it a positive one. I do hope these books encourage children and parents to talk about these sometimes difficult issues. Talking together goes a long way to finding a solution.

Sarah

Sarah, Duchess of York

Zach loved television, computers, and books. His idea of the perfect day was to sit at home and do all three! He would even try and take a book with him during recess at school.

Zach didn't have many friends because he preferred to play games or read alone. He didn't get much exercise sitting on the couch in front of the TV.

Zach's mom and dad sometimes worried about him. They reminded Zach that he should get some exercise every day, but Zach didn't really want to.

Even Dad sits in front of the TV when he comes home from work most days, Zach thought.

Every week, Zach tried to
get out of going to gym class at school.
He hated gym! One morning, he asked his mom to write
him an excuse note.

"Mom, I'm not as good as the other kids at any sports. I
don't even want to try," Zach said.

"You need to attend every class at school, Zach. Not just
the ones you like," she explained gently.

Zach's mom would not write the excuse note to his gym
teacher, which made him mad!

The next day, Zach and his mom heard a lot of noise coming from the house next door. Furniture was being unloaded from a big van outside.

"Look, Zach!" said his mom. "New neighbors just moved in next door."

Zach was playing a computer game and didn't hear what his mom had said.

Later, when Zach's mom walked to the mailbox, she saw a woman cleaning the windows of the house next door.

"Hello! You must be our new neighbors. Welcome! Why don't you come around this afternoon for a visit?" asked Zach's mom.

"Thank you. I'd love to," said the woman. "May I bring Michael, my son?"

"Of course. He can meet Zach," she replied.

Michael and his mom visited later that afternoon.

Zach asked Michael, "Do you want to play a computer game?"

Michael agreed, and soon they were both playing—and Zach was winning!

After three or four games, Michael said, "Come on, Zach. Let's go for a bike ride. You can show me around the neighborhood."

Zach frowned. His bike was rusty and had flat tires. He also didn't really know any places to go in the neighborhood.

"Sorry, I can't," he said, embarrassed.

Early the next morning, Zach's mom told him to take out the trash. He didn't want to do it. All he wanted to do was lay on his bed watching cartoons.

Zach grumbled all the way to the curb—until he saw Michael outside his house.

"What is your favorite cartoon? My favorite is on TV right now. Want to watch it with me?" Zach asked Michael.

"I can't," said Michael. "Mom and I are taking Turnip for his first walk around our new neighborhood. Would you like to come with us?"

"Turnip?" asked Zach, "I thought turnips were something you ate, not something you take for a walk."

"This Turnip is my Yorkshire Terrier," said Michael. "I walk him every day."

"Walking is boring," said Zach. "TV is more fun."

"But we are going to the park where there are lots of fun things to do," said Michael.

"That's less boring, I guess," said Zach. He wanted to watch TV, but he wanted to play with Michael more. Zach walked back to the house and called out to his mom.

"I'm going for a walk with Michael and Turnip," said Zach.

His mom looked shocked!

The park was huge. Zach had only been there once before. They found lots of sticks for Turnip to chase after. In the corner was a big, old tree.

"Come on!" said Michael. "Let's see who can climb the highest."

Michael climbed higher than Zach, but they both had a great time. They laughed when Turnip stood at the bottom of the tree, barking at them until they came down.

On the way home, Zach said to Michael, "I had fun today with you and Turnip. Can I come to the park with you again?"

"What are you doing on Sunday?" asked Michael. "My friend Grace is coming over and we are going to ride our bikes there. You could come, too."

Zach said he'd love to.

Sunday was a beautiful day. Zach cleaned off his bike and took it to Michael's house where Grace met them. The three children set off together on their bikes.

Michael was in the lead. Grace pedaled hard to keep up with him, and Zach puffed along last.

"Come on, Zach," said Michael. "Catch up with us!"

Zach realized that if he put in a little more effort, he would soon be riding as fast as his new friends. It was a great feeling and he was really enjoying himself!

When Zach came home that evening, his mom said, "You've got rosy cheeks!" and pinched them.

Zach had to admit he felt good—tired, but good. He was so tired, in fact, that he missed his favorite TV show that night.

When Zach's dad heard about his day, he told Zach about how he used to ride a bike when he was younger.

"You should come with me next time!" said Zach.

Over the next few weeks, Zach and Michael became close friends. They played indoors and out. Now and then, they would watch television or play games together on the computer. But Zach no longer won the computer games all the time and Michael didn't always climb trees the fastest.

Zach and his dad also rode bikes together. Zach always took the lead—but his dad was definitely catching up!

TEN HELPFUL HINTS
FOR PARENTS TO KEEP THEIR CHILDREN ACTIVE
By Dr. Richard Woolfson, PhD

1. Build physical activity into your child's normal daily routine. Rather than making exercise something out-of-the-ordinary for your child, encourage him to walk to school, play outdoors, or ride his bike.

2. Set a good example yourself. If you follow a healthy lifestyle, your child will follow suit. Good habits established in childhood will last into adulthood.

3. Make physical exercise fun. For example, there is no reason why walking, jogging, or biking can't be part of a family outing to somewhere special.

4. Try to limit the amount of time your child spends sitting in front of the computer or television. Agree to a daily limit for these activities and ensure your child sticks to it.

5. Suggest after-school activities. Physical exercise is included in many activities, not just sports. For instance, dance and drama classes include movement. Your child will also enjoy making new friends while pursuing these activities.

6. Make sure that your child participates in gym class in school. She needs to know that you expect her to join in and that you won't help her to avoid it.

7. Find out about local recreational centers, sports teams, and activity clubs and then discuss them with your child. Suggest that he tries at least one of these in his area. Let him choose which one to join.

8. Give her active household chores, such as taking out the garbage, raking leaves in the yard, or washing the family car. Every bit of exercise helps.

9. Emphasize the benefits of exercise to your child. Explain to him that it keeps his body healthy, and gives him good muscles and strong bones.

10. Buy toys that require physical activity. A bat and ball, a tennis racket, a jungle gym, a small trampoline for the yard, or a swing set are all popular toys that encourage exercise.

Dr. Richard Woolfson is a child psychologist, working with children and their families. He is also an author and has written several books on child development and family life, in addition to numerous articles for magazines and newspapers. Dr. Woolfson runs training workshops for parents and child care professionals and appears regularly on radio and television. He is a Fellow of the British Psychological Society.

Helping Hand Books

Look for these other helpful books to share with your child:

Ashley Learns About Strangers

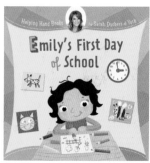
Emily's First Day of School

Michael and His New Baby Brother

Matthew and the Bullies

When Katie's Parents Separated

Jacob Goes to the Doctor and Sophie Visits the Dentist

Molly makes Friends

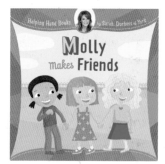
Olivia says Goodbye to Grandpa

Healthy Food for Dylan

Get Well Soon Adam

Lauren's Moving Day